DEAR READER,

We're excited to present this book to you as a gift from us to take home, read and enjoy.

Imagination can lead to endless possibilities and reading stories about interesting characters and far-off lands is a great way to encourage children to explore and imagine new things. That is exactly what this book, *Boy Soup,* does. The Giant's Home Medical Guide says that a big bowl of Boy Soup is the cure for a giant with a gigantic cold. To make the soup the giant will need to catch a big batch of boys for the pot. While the boys are easy for the giant to catch and add to the pot, the giant also catches a girl named Kate who has a very different recipe for this giant's bowl of soup.

As part of many children's reading programs we support each year, all of us at TD are proud to provide this book to you as part of the TD Grade One Book Giveaway. Every Grade One student in Canada will receive their very own copy of *Boy Soup* this year. Remember, imagination can take you to new places, so continue to discover the magical world of books by visiting your local library.

Have fun reading!

Ed Clark
Group President and CEO
TD Bank Group

For more information on all TD supported reading initiatives, see
www.tdreads.com

DEAR STUDENTS AND PARENTS:

The Canadian Children's Book Centre is proud to partner with TD Bank Group to give you *Boy Soup*, this year's selection, as part of the National TD Grade One Book Giveaway Program.

Please take the book home with you to read with your parents. We think you will all love this story of a girl who saves her friends from ending up as the main ingredient for a soup that an ogre thinks will help him to get rid of his cold!

We hope that you and your parents will also take the time to read some of the great Canadian, award-winning books listed in the back of this book. For more information on and access to resources on programs promoting reading, go to **www.bookcentre.ca** and **www.tdreads.com**.

Happy reading!

Charlotte Teeple

Charlotte Teeple
Executive Director
The Canadian Children's Book Centre

The Canadian Children's Book Centre

THE CANADIAN CHILDREN'S BOOK CENTRE

Over 500,000 Grade One students across Canada will receive a copy of this book, *Boy Soup*, through the annual **TD Grade One Book Giveaway Program,** administered by the Canadian Children's Book Centre (CCBC) and funded by TD Bank Group.

The Canadian Children's Book Centre is a national, not-for-profit organization that promotes the reading, writing and illustrating of Canadian children's books. The CCBC provides programs, resources, materials and activities that are used by teachers, librarians, authors, illustrators, publishers, booksellers and parents.

Best Books for Kids & Teens is the CCBC's semi-annual selection guide to the best new Canadian books, magazines, audio and video. Each year, hundreds of recently-published books and other resources are evaluated and selected by jury committees from across the country. *Best Books for Kids & Teens* highlights the best Canadian books to buy, borrow and read, making it a terrific resource for anyone who wants to make informed selections for young readers.

Canadian Children's Book News, the CCBC's quarterly magazine, reviews books, interviews authors and illustrators, profiles publishers and bookstores, informs and updates readers about issues affecting children's education and reading and provides information and news about the world of children's books in Canada.

The CCBC organizes **TD Canadian Children's Book Week**, the largest annual celebration of Canadian books and readings in schools and libraries across Canada. Each spring, Canadian authors, illustrators and storytellers travel across the country, from coast to coast and up to the Arctic, visiting schools, libraries, community centres and bookstores to talk about their books with young readers. TD Book Week also inspires many independent activities and local celebrations of Canadian children's books and their creators.

The CCBC coordinates **six major children's literature awards** with cash prizes totalling over $130,000, including the **TD Canadian Children's Literature Award** for the most distinguished English and French-language books of the year, the **Marilyn Baillie Picture Book Award** for the best picture book of the year, the **Norma Fleck Award for Canadian Children's Non-Fiction**, the **Geoffrey Bilson Award for Historical Fiction for Young People**, the **John Spray Mystery Award** for the best mystery book of the year and the **Monica Hughes Award for Science Fiction and Fantasy**.

For more information on the Canadian Children's Book Centre and the TD Grade One Book Giveaway Program, please visit our website at **www.bookcentre.ca**.

The Canadian Children's Book Centre
Bringing Canadian books and young readers together

The Canadian Children's Book Centre
40 Orchard View Blvd., Suite 217, Toronto, Ontario M4R 1B9
Telephone: 416 975-0010, Fax: 416 975-8970, Email: info@bookcentre.ca

Special edition prepared for the TD Grade One Book Giveaway Program.

This edition is published by special arrangement with the Canadian Children's Book Centre and TD Bank Group for free distribution to Grade One children across Canada.

To "The Goup"

The Canadian Children's Book Centre
Suite 217, 40 Orchard View Blvd.
Toronto, Ontario M4R 1B9
www.bookcentre.ca

Annick Press
15 Patricia Avenue
Toronto, Ontario M2M 1H9
www.annickpress.com

Printed and bound in Canada by Friesens Corporation
Also available in French: *La soupe de garçons*
ISBN (English) 978-0-929095-84-4
ISBN (French) 978-0-929095-86-8

Library and Archives Canada Cataloguing in Publication

Lesynski, Loris
      Boy soup / written by Loris Lesynski ; illustrated by Michael Martchenko.

"This edition is published by special arrangement with the Canadian Children's
      Book Centre and TD Bank Group for free distribution to grade one children
      across Canada".
ISBN 978-0-929095-84-4

      I. Martchenko, Michael II. Canadian Children's Book Centre III. Title.

PS8573.E79B69 2013   jC813'.54   C2013-902008-X

BOY SOUP

Written by Loris Lesynski

Illustrated by Michael Martchenko

annick press

Toronto • New York • Vancouver

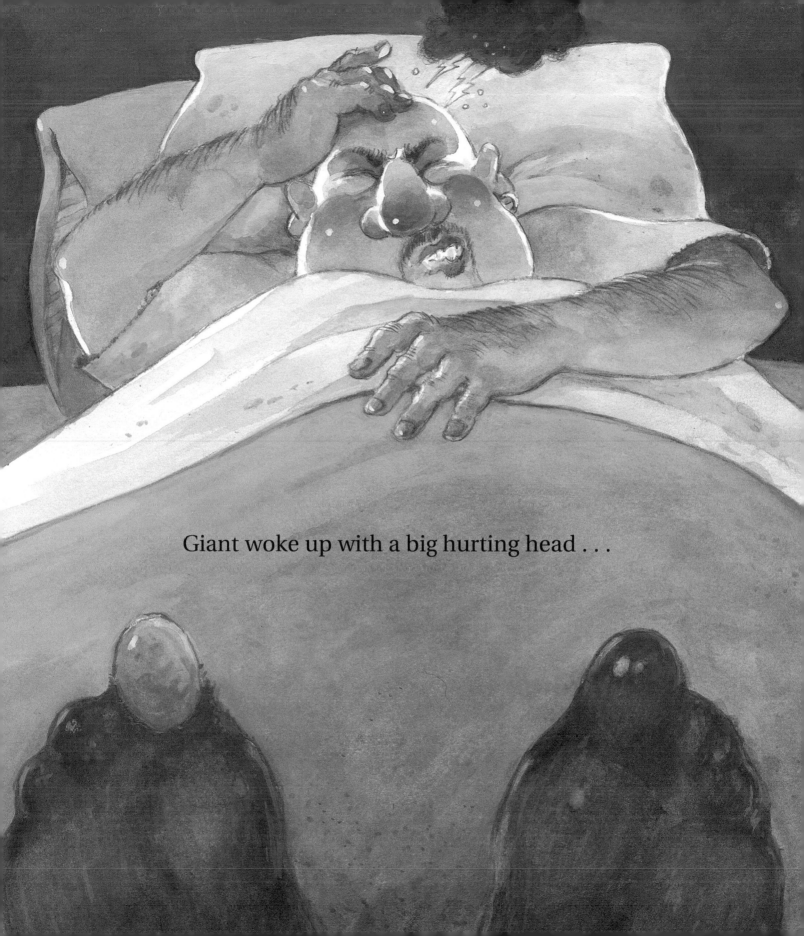

Giant woke up with a big hurting head . . .

"I am sore I am sick I feel awful," he said.

He coughed—
    moving mountains.
He hacked—
    causing quakes.
He said with a whimper,
    "My everything aches."

Groaning, he shovelled his blankets aside
    and reached for his *Giants
    Home Medical Guide*.

With sofa-sized fingers,
  he leafed through the book,
and in between sneezes
  so loud that he shook,
he found all his symptoms—
  page seventy-one:

"Queasiness,
  wheeziness,
  coughing begun.
  Completely depleted
  and tending to droop."

The only prescription?

"A bowl of
Boy Soup."

"Can't *be*," said the giant. "Would be a disgrace."
    But a big greedy grin spread all over his face.

"Of course, if I'm ill, that's a decent excuse.
    And think of the broth
        a good boy could produce.
    A sweet boy, a neat boy,
        a boy so delicious
    a giant might find himself
        licking the dishes . . .

One buttery boy—or better, a group.
    A half-dozen lads would make
        wonderful soup!"

Catching the boys was as easy as pie:
   he stretched down his thick giant arm through the sky
and rested his hand at the top of a tree
    where children were playing—they just didn't see
      the branch they were grabbing
          could grab *them*.
                    Too late!

That's how the giant got five boys—
and Kate.

"Why *should* I feel guilty?"
the giant began
when six angry children
protested his plan.

"It's here in this authorized
medical book!"

Kate asked, "Before supper,
could *I* have a look?"

She read every word
in the faded ink
and said, "May I have
just a minute to think?"

—but "**NO!**" snapped the giant. "Boys, *into* the pot!
  I've chills and a fever,
    I'm cold and I'm hot."
      And then with a thunderous splat blew his nose
        as the boys shook with fear
          from their heads to their toes.

        Kate racked her brain at a furious rate
          to save all her friends from this hideous fate.

        The giant was ready.

        How could they flee?

Their ten rubber running shoes—
that was the key!

Just as the giant came closer to scoop
    the lads for his horrid medicinal soup,
Kate gave a signal, the tiniest look.
    The boys understood.
They leapt to the book
                and started a dance, half a shuffle, half-run,
                    and jogged back and forth on page seventy-one.
                            Up the page, *down* the page,
                                sidestep, repeat—

—'til most
  of each word
    was erased
      by their feet.

"Now I can't check it!"
the giant complained.
But Kate said, "I've read it,
I'll gladly explain.
The book said quite clearly,
of this I am sure—
Boy Soup is soup *made* by boys,
that's the cure."

"But . . ." sniffed the giant,
"I thought boys went *in* it . . .
I think I'm confused . . .
can you give me a minute?"

"Oh, no," Kate proclaimed. "You're too sick, don't you know.
We have to work fast. Come on, fellows, let's go!"

The boys cooked the carrots ✓
  the boys boiled the peas ✓
then seasoned the soup
  with a handful of fleas ✓

They put in
  some mud ✓
  some thick yellow glue ✓
  and a generous dollop of dandruff shampoo ✓

Kate poured in
  pepper ✓
  red hot sauce ✓
  really, really, really, *really* rotten bananas ✓
  and candy floss ✓
  sour green pickles ✓
  and beans in the can ✓
—all simmered together
  as part of the plan.

And oh, the aroma!
  Like skunk in a pot.

  Kate smiled her sweetest
    and served it up hot.

In between snuffles, the giant took sips
        from a spoon trembling close
            to his great hairy lips.

He scowled in suspicion but took one more taste
        with a huge doughy tongue much the colour of paste—

then tipped the whole potful of soup down his throat
        . . . sat back
            . . . and *sighed*
                —'til he started to bloat!

And the pepper, the mud, and the pickles
            combined.

The giant let out a most terrible whine—

—and SPIT out the soup
with so mighty a blast
that it blew
all the children
down homeward at last.

Kate and the fellows
    were dented, but sound,
when they landed back
    home on familiar ground . . .

They needed new sneakers,
and something to do
to get over the horrible shock
they'd been through.

The *giant* was not
who they wanted to feed.
But they *had* liked the cooking,
with Kate in the lead.

So they opened Boys' Restaurant
as a group
—and served almost everything
but Boy Soup.

One day at the diner, delivery came
of an extra-large envelope bearing Kate's name.

The giant had written:

I *did* get your letter.
Thank you for asking,
I *am* feeling better.

That Medical Book is from long, long ago.
They boiled little boys then,
even though
you're *RIGHT* that it's wrong—
I guess that I knew it—
but feeling so sick made me tempted
to do it.
I'm *glad* that you tricked me.
I would have felt bad
when later I realized
I'd eaten a lad.

I told all the giants:
no Boy Soup for me!

Sorry again.

Yours sincerely,

Big G.

LORIS LESYNSKI

MICHAEL MARTCHENKO

From her very first picture book, the wildly popular *Boy Soup* (1996) to her most recent book of poems, *Crazy About Soccer!* (2012), Loris Lesynski's name has become synonymous with poetry for kids. Loris's love of language combined with a keen sense of humour and a natural gift for rhythm and rhyme have resulted in a dozen lively, funny books enjoyed by children everywhere.

Ever since she was a young girl, Loris enjoyed writing stories, which she also illustrated. Once her books started to be published, Loris discovered that she loved talking to teachers and librarians about how to get young people excited about poetry. She has visited many classrooms where she shares with children her ideas about writing, drawing, and publishing. Loris is never happier than when she sees kids get inspired to write their own poems or stories after one of her visits.

As the illustrator of one of the most popular children's books ever written, *The Paper Bag Princess*, Michael Martchenko's art is recognized throughout the world.

Before he became a children's book illustrator, Michael had already launched a successful career in advertising. Fortunately for fans of children's literature, the publishers at Annick Press and Robert Munsch saw Michael's work at a graphic arts exhibition, and felt that anyone with such a playful imagination should illustrate children's stories. Since then, Michael has illustrated over 30 books for children, including such Munsch classics as *Thomas' Snowsuit*, *Mortimer*, and *The Fire Station*.

Growing up in a small town north of Paris, France, Michael loved comic books and learned a lot about visual humor from watching cartoons. He moved to Canada when he was seven. By high school, he knew that he wanted to make art his career.

Watch a brief movie with the author Loris Lesynski and illustrator Michael Martchenko showing how the book was made.
www.tdreads.com/BoySoup

2012 AWARD-WINNING CANADIAN CHILDREN'S BOOKS

Dear Reader: Here are some other great Canadian children's books.
The ones with a star (★) are suitable for readers ages 4 to 7.

ALBERTA CHILDREN'S AND YOUNG ADULT BOOK OF THE YEAR AWARD
Wayne Lynch. *Canadian Rockies Wildlife for Kids.* Banff, AB: Summerthought Publishing, 2011.

ALCUIN SOCIETY AWARDS FOR EXCELLENCE IN BOOK DESIGN IN CANADA
★ David Weale. *Doors in the Air.* Illustrated by Pierre Pratt. Designer: Teresa Bubela. Victoria: Orca Book Publishers, 2012.

AMELIA FRANCES HOWARD-GIBBON ILLUSTRATOR'S AWARD
★ Matthew Forsythe. *My Name Is Elizabeth!* by Annika Dunklee. Toronto: Kids Can Press, 2011.

ANN CONNOR BRIMER AWARD FOR CHILDREN'S LITERATURE
Susan White. *The Year Mrs. Montague Cried.* Charlottetown: The Acorn Press, 2011.

ARTHUR ELLIS BEST JUVENILE CRIME AWARD
Tim Wynne-Jones. *Blink & Caution.* Somerville, MA: Candlewick Press, 2011.

BLUE SPRUCE AWARD
★ Rebecca Bender. *Giraffe and Bird.* Toronto: Dancing Cat Books, 2010.

BMO WINTERSET AWARD
★ Andy Jones. *Jack & Mary in the Land of Thieves.* Illustrated by Darka Erdelji. St. John's: Running the Goat Books & Broadsides, 2012.

BOLEN BOOKS CHILDREN'S BOOK PRIZE
Caitlyn Vernon. *Nowhere Else on Earth: Standing Tall for the Great Bear Rainforest.* Victoria: Orca Book Publishers, 2011.

CANADIAN LIBRARY ASSOCIATION BOOK OF THE YEAR FOR CHILDREN AWARD
Kit Pearson. *The Whole Truth.* Toronto: HarperCollins Publishers, 2011.

CANADIAN LIBRARY ASSOCIATION YOUNG ADULT BOOK AWARD
Catherine Austen. *All Good Children.* Victoria: Orca Book Publishers, 2011.

CBA LIBRIS AWARD
★ (Picture Book) Barbara Reid. *Picture a Tree.* Toronto: North Winds Press/Scholastic Canada, 2011.
(Young Readers) Kenneth Oppel. *This Dark Endeavour: The Apprenticeship of Victor Frankenstein.* Toronto: HarperCollins Publishers, 2011.

CHOCOLATE LILY YOUNG READERS' CHOICE AWARD
★ (Picture Book) Linda Bailey. *Stanley's Little Sister.* Illustrated by Bill Slavin. Toronto: Kids Can Press, 2010.
(Chapter Book) Michelle Superle. *Black Dog Dream Dog.* Illustrated by Millie Ballance. Vancouver: Tradewind Books, 2010.
(Novel) Beryl Young. *Follow the Elephant.* Vancouver: Ronsdale Press, 2010.

CHRISTIE HARRIS ILLUSTRATED CHILDREN'S LITERATURE PRIZE
★ Sara O'Leary. *When I Was Small.* Illustrated by Julie Morstad. Vancouver: Simply Read Books, 2011.

DIAMOND WILLOW AWARD
Becky Citra. *Missing.* Victoria: Orca Book Publishers, 2011.

ELIZABETH MRAZIK-CLEAVER AWARD
★ Isabelle Arsenault. *Virginia Wolf* by Kyo Maclear. Toronto: Kids Can Press, 2012.

FIRST NATION COMMUNITIES READ
Janet Wilson. *Shannen and the Dream for a School.* Toronto: Second Story Press, 2011.

GEOFFREY BILSON AWARD FOR HISTORICAL FICTION FOR YOUNG PEOPLE
Kate Cayley. *The Hangman in the Mirror.* Toronto: Annick Press, 2011.